WITHDRAWN

THE MAN WHO MARRIED
 A DUMB WIFE

"Good gentlemen and ladies, we pray you to forgive the author all his faults."
(See page 93)

THE
MAN WHO MARRIED
A DUMB WIFE

A COMEDY IN TWO ACTS

BY

ANATOLE FRANCE

Of the French Academy

TRANSLATED FOR MR. GRANVILLE BARKER

BY

CURTIS HIDDEN PAGE

Translator of Molière and Ronsard

EIGHT ILLUSTRATIONS
FROM PHOTOGRAPHS

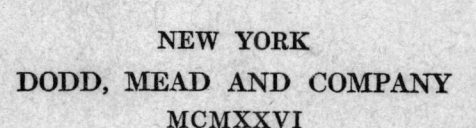

NEW YORK
DODD, MEAD AND COMPANY
MCMXXVI

COPYRIGHT, 1915, BY JOHN LANE COMPANY

All rights reserved, including rights of production and adaptation. The dramatic rights are controlled by Mr. Granville Barker. Application for the right of production, whether amateur or professional, should be made to Dodd, Mead and Company, 449 Fourth Avenue, New York City.

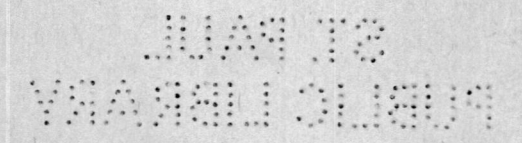

PRINTED IN U. S. A.

TO
LILLAH McCARTHY
AND
GRANVILLE BARKER

INTRODUCTION

The comedy of "The Man Who Married a Dumb Wife" was written, or at least begun, merely to entertain the members of the "Society of Rabelaisian Studies" at one of their meetings. But it succeeded so well that it was at once taken up by a regular theatre, the Porte-Saint-Martin, in the spring of 1912, and again at the Théâtre de la Renaissance in the autumn.

It is founded on a brief passage in the "Lives, Heroick Deeds, and Sayings of Gargantua and His Son Pantagruel," where one of Rabelais' characters tells of a joyous incident in his student days at the University of Montpellier. This can best be given in the rich and racy old English translation by Sir Thomas Urquhart, who, in translating, somewhat enlarges on Rabelais' version.

" 'Welcome, in good faith, my dear master, welcome! It did me good to hear you talk, the

Lord be praised for all. I do not remember to have seen you before now, since the last time that you acted at Montpellier with our ancient friends, Anthony Saporra, Guy Bourguyer, Balthasar Noyer, Tolet, John Quentin, Francis Robinet, John Perdrier and Francis Rabelais, the moral comedy of him who had espoused and married a dumb wife.'

" 'I was there,' quoth Epistemon. 'The good, honest man, her husband, was very earnestly urgent to have the fillet of her tongue untied, and would needs have her speak by any means. At his desire some pains were taken on her, and partly by the industry of the physician, other part by the expertness of the surgeon, the encyliglotte which she had under her tongue being cut, she spoke, and spoke again; yea, within a few hours she spoke so loud, so much, so fiercely, and so long, that her poor husband returned to the same physician for a recipe to make her hold her peace. "There are," quoth the physician, "many proper remedies in our art to make dumb women speak, but there are none that ever I could learn therein to make them silent. The only cure which I have found out is their husbands' deafness." The wretch

MONSIEUR ANATOLE FRANCE

became within a few weeks thereafter, by virtue of some drugs, charms or enchantments, which the physician had prescribed unto him, so deaf, that he could not have heard the thundering of nineteen hundred cannons at a salvo. His wife, perceiving that indeed he was deaf as a doornail, and that her scolding was but in vain, sith that he heard her not, she grew stark mad.'

" 'Then, the doctor asking for his fee, the husband answered that truly he was deaf, and so was not able to understand what the tenour of this demand might be. Whereupon the leech bedusted him with a little, I know not what, sort of powder, which rendered him a fool immediately, so great was the stultificating virtue of that strange kind of pulverised dose. Then did this fool of a husband and his mad wife join together, and, falling on the doctor and the surgeon, did so scratch, bethwack, and bang them, that they were left half dead upon the place, so furious were the blows which they received. I never in all my lifetime laughed so much as at the acting of that buffoonery.' "

It was probably this brief passage in Rabelais that suggested to Molière, who knew his Rabelais thoroughly, two of the best scenes in the third act of his "Doctor by Compulsion." But Molière has entirely changed the characters, their relations to each other, and the whole setting of the incident; he has made the dumb wife into a daughter, who only pretends to have been struck dumb temporarily in order to escape from marriage with a rich old man. The pretended doctor, who "cures" her, is a secret agent of her lover, whom he brings along with him disguised as an apothecary. But Molière uses to full advantage the situation after the "cure"; for the young lady recovers her speech only to assert that she will have none of the old man, that she will marry no one except her Lysander, that she will on no consideration obey her father or even for a moment listen to him; she speaks, "so loud, so much, so fiercely, and so long," that her father in despair calls on the doctor to make her dumb again, only to receive the same answer as the husband in Rabelais' story.

Whether there ever existed such a play as Rabelais describes and Molière imitates—whether Rabelais drew the story from his capacious memory or from his equally capacious and riotously creative imagination—can prob-

INTRODUCTION

ably never be known. But there ought to have been such a play; it might even serve as a perfect type of the mediæval drama; it is actually *needed* by the scholarly seekers after Molière's and Rabelais' sources! And since, if it ever existed, it has now been lost, Monsieur Anatole France has been good enough to re-create it for us.

Monsieur France is not primarily a dramatist. In fact, in his abundant production of many kinds, there are in all only three or four brief plays. But in whatever he turns his hand to he is always a clever craftsman and a master of French style at its best—which is, of course, the best in the world. And whether he is writing a novel, or sketches of provincial or Parisian manners, or politics, or criticism, or incidentally turning to modern or mediæval drama, he is always a satirist of society and a sociable satirist.

In "The Man Who Married a Dumb Wife" his social satire is thoroughly up-to-date, dealing as it does with subjects which are "of all time," such as the high cost of living, the servant problem, the tendency to extravagance, the fashions of to-day and to-morrow, the wisdom, and the pretensions to wisdom, of the medical profession, the loquacity of the ladies, and so on and so on—it is remarkable how much he has got in, and how little he has left out. Much of it is done in the broad, mediæval manner, as when he exhibits the enormous surgical instruments of the doctors who take good care "not to be caught unarmed by a patient," or when he follows with entire faithfulness the simple outlines of the plot as given by Rabelais; but everything is as delicately worked out in detail as Monsieur France's own work cannot help being. He has used the language of to-day, without any artificial help from the "marry-come-up, 'sblood, 'sdeath, and go-to" style, which our too easily historical novelists and dramatists so blithely resort to; yet he has perfectly reproduced the tone and spirit of mediæval comedy.

It should be added that Mr. Granville Barker in his production has achieved exactly the same kind of doubly artistic effect, in his broad, simple outlining of the whole conception and decoration, and his minute and delicate attention to every detail of the groupings, intonations, costumes, postures, and colouring. The "dec-

INTRODUCTION

oration," designed by Mr. Robert E. Jones, has been best described by Mr. A. H. Woollcott:

> "What you see in the single setting is the front of Master Botal's house, looking out toward the . . . but was the Pont-Neuf built then? Your view is of the interior of one of the rooms and of the street in front. It is a gray and black background, simple, flat, slightly conventionalized in design, and unobtrusively serviceable to the movement of the quaintly clad figures in front of it, and to the splotches of plain, vivid colouring that the costuming involves. All these are right and contributory, from the black hose of the agile and amative secretary to the buttercup gown of *Mistress So and So* who goes mincing insufferably by, with her lackey literally dancing attendance. Robert E. Jones, the young American disciple of the 'new school,' who did the decorations, is to be congratulated. What is produced by his work and by every line and posture of the play—the contributions are indistinguishable—is a rich flavour of fanciful mediævalism."

Every detail of the movements of the characters against this background has been planned even more carefully than is usual in good dramatic production, so that at any and every moment when the spectator thinks of looking for it he will find a well-composed picture on the stage. Yet the rollicking farce-comedy seems to go all the more rapidly for this careful planning. I have tried to carry over into the printed text some sense of these details, without too much slowing-up the movement or blurring the picture, by giving enough additional stage directions adapted from Mr. Barker's prompt-book, to suggest the manner of production. All such additions to M. Anatole France's text are enclosed in parentheses.

It only remains to express my hearty thanks to Mr. Barker both for the use of his prompt-book and for many other generous courtesies; and to Mr. Cecil Sharp for his kind permission to print the music which he has so aptly adapted to the songs and street-cries.

C. H. P.

MR. GRANVILLE BARKER

ILLUSTRATIONS

FACING PAGE

"Good gentlemen and ladies, we pray you to forgive the author all his faults" . . . *Frontispiece*

Monsieur Anatole France 8

Mr. Granville Barker 14

"Enter Catherine" 36

"Now we are here, shall we go see the patient?" 46

"Mademoiselle, you arouse my interest" . 72

" 'Tis delicious! I can't hear a thing" . 90

"Oh! She has bitten me!" 92

PROPERTY PLOT

Doctor's Telescope
Gilded Flasks
Gilded Glasses on wooden Tray
Curtains to work
Books
Bookcase
Parchments
Distaff on Bookcase
Tome
Red Step-Ladder
1 Chair
2 Baskets for Alison with Chianti Bottles
Gold Cloth (draped over balcony)
Table with white Cover
Black Quill
Inkwell
A Chickweed Basket
A Watercress Basket
Cane for Blind Man
Cane for Maugie
Case containing four large instruments
Form in front of Table
12-ft. Bench below Balcony
Covered Basket
Sand Box
Water Pitcher
Rebeck and Bow
1 Broom for Sweep
Spectacles
Candles on a String
Statement for Fumée
Tapestry Frame
Gilded Vial for Powder

*First Production for the Stage Society,
Wallack's Theatre, New York City,
January 26, 1915.*

DRAMATIS PERSONÆ

Master Leonard Botal, *Judge*	O. P. Heggie
Master Adam Fumée, *Lawyer*	Edgar Kent
Master Simon Colline, *Doctor*	Arnold Lucy
Master Jean Maugier, *Surgeon*	Lionel Braham
Master Serafin Dulaurier, *Apothecary*	Ernest Cossart
Giles Boiscourtier, *Secretary*	Horace Braham
A Blind Fiddler	Cecil Cameron
Catherine, *Botal's Wife*	Lillah McCarthy
Alison, *Botal's Servant*	Eva Leonard-Boyne
Mademoiselle de la Garandière	Isabel Jeans
Madame de la Bruine	Ruby Blyth
The Chickweed Man	Edgar Roberts
The Watercress Man	Gerald Hamer
The Candle Man	Hugh McRae
Page to Mademoiselle de la Garandière	Edmond Banks
Footman to Madame de la Bruine	Manice Lewis
First Doctor's Attendant	Richard Cort
Second Doctor's Attendant	Gerald Gardener

PERSONS OF THE PLAY

MASTER LEONARD BOTAL, *Judge.*
MASTER ADAM FUMÉE, *Lawyer.*
MASTER SIMON COLLINE, *Doctor.*
MASTER JEAN MAUGIER, *Surgeon and Barber.*
MASTER SERAFIN DULAURIER, *Apothecary.*
GILES BOISCOURTIER, *Leonard Botal's Secretary.*
A BLIND MAN.
CATHERINE, *Leonard Botal's wife.*
ALISON, *Leonard Botal's servant.*
MADEMOISELLE DE LA GARANDIÈRE.

THE MAN WHO MARRIED A DUMB WIFE

ACT I

A large room in JUDGE LEONARD BOTAL'S *house, at Paris.*
Left: Main entrance, from the rue Dauphine; when the door is open, vista to the Pont-Neuf.
Right: Door to the kitchen.
At the rear of the stage: A wooden stairway, leading to the upper rooms.
On the walls are portraits of magistrates, in gown and wig, and along the walls, great cabinets, or cupboards, full of books, papers, parchments, and bags of legal documents, with more piled on top of the cabinets. There is a double stepladder on castors, with flat steps on

each side, used to reach the top of the cabinets.

A writing table, small chairs, upholstered arm-chairs, and a spinning-wheel.

(In Mr. Granville Barker's production, the street is shown in front of the house, instead of being concealed behind it; so that the chimney-sweep, the chickweed-seller, the candle-man, etc., pass across the front of the stage.

The street door of the house opens on a hall-way, from which a door leads off to the kitchen, and a short stairway leads up, in a direction parallel with the front of the stage, past a double lattice window open to the street, to an upper room in which most of the action takes place.

This room has a large balcony and window-seat, and stands entirely open to the street. The writing-table, bookcase (instead of cabinets), and stepladder are seen within it. There is a bench or form, long enough to seat two or three people, in front of the table. A door at the right rear corner of the room is supposed to open on a stairway leading to the rooms above.)

Scene I

Giles Boiscourtier, Alison; later Master Adam Fumée and Master Leonard Botal.

(Giles is discovered sitting on a small form in front of the table; on the rise of the curtain he turns to the audience, bows in flamboyant style, and then sits down again, with his back to the audience.

The Chickweed Man *goes by, calling:* "Chickweed! Chickweed! Good birdseed, good birdseed, good birdseed for saäle!"

Enter Alison, *with a large basket under each arm. She curtsies to the audience.* Giles, *as soon as he spies her, runs to the street door and stands quiet beside it, so that she does not notice him. As she starts to enter the house, he jumps at her and snatches a bottle from one of the baskets.)*

ALISON

Holy Mary, don't you know better than to jump at anybody like a bogie-man, right here in a public place?

GILES

[*Pulling a bottle of wine out of the other basket.*]

Don't scream, you little goose. Nobody's going to pluck you. You're not worth it.

(*Enter* MASTER ADAM FUMÉE. *He bows to the audience.*)

ALISON

Will you let the Judge's wine alone, you rascal!

[*She sets down her baskets, snatches back one of the bottles, cuffs the secretary, picks up her baskets, and goes off to the kitchen. The kitchen fire-place is seen through the half-open door.*]

MASTER ADAM

(*Slightly formal in manner and speech at first.*)

A DUMB WIFE

Is this the dwelling of Mr. Leonard Botal, Judge in civil and criminal cases?

GILES

(With bottle behind his back, and bowing.)
Yes, sir; it's here, sir; and I'm his secretary, Giles Boiscourtier, at your service, sir.

MASTER ADAM

Then, boy, go tell him his old school-fellow, Master Adam Fumée, lawyer, wishes to see him on business.

GILES

Here he comes now, sir.
 [LEONARD BOTAL *comes down the stairs.* GILES *goes off into the kitchen.*]

MASTER ADAM

Good day, Master Leonard Botal, I am delighted to see you again.

LEONARD

Good morning, Master Adam Fumée, how have you been this long time that I haven't set eyes on you?

MASTER ADAM

Well, very well. And I hope I find you the same, your Honour.

LEONARD

Fairly so, fairly so. And what good wind wafts you hither, Master Adam Fumée?
(They come forward in the room.)

MASTER ADAM

I've come from Chartres on purpose to put in your own hands a statement on behalf of a young orphan girl . . .

LEONARD

Master Adam Fumée, do you remember the days when we were law students together at Orleans University?

MASTER ADAM

Yes, yes; we used to play the flute together, and take the ladies out to picnics, and dance from morning to night. . . But I've come, your Honour, my dear old school-fellow, to hand you

A DUMB WIFE

a statement on behalf of a young orphan girl whose case is now pending before you.

LEONARD

Will she give good fees?

MASTER ADAM

She is a young orphan girl . . .

LEONARD

Yes, yes, I know. But, will she give good fees?

MASTER ADAM

She is a young orphan girl, who's been robbed by her guardian, and he left her nothing but her eyes to weep with. But if she wins her suit, she will be rich again, and will give plentiful proof of her gratitude.

LEONARD

[*Taking the statement which Master Adam hands him.*]
We will look into the matter.

MASTER ADAM

I thank you, your Honour, my dear old school-fellow.

LEONARD

We will look into it, without fear or favour.

MASTER ADAM

That goes without saying. . . . But, tell me: Is everything going smoothly with you? You seem worried. And yet, you are well placed here . . . the judgeship's a good one?

LEONARD

I paid enough for it to be a good one—and I didn't get cheated.

MASTER ADAM

Perhaps you are lonely. Why don't you get married?

LEONARD

What, what! Don't you know, Master Adam, that I *have* just been married? *(They sit down on the form in front of the table.)* Yes, only last month, to a girl from one of our

A DUMB WIFE

best country families, young and handsome, Catherine Momichel, the seventh daughter of the Criminal Court Judge at Salency. But alas! she is dumb. Now you know my affliction.

MASTER ADAM

Your wife is dumb?

LEONARD

Alas, yes.

MASTER ADAM

Quite, quite dumb?

LEONARD

As a fish.

MASTER ADAM

And you didn't notice it till after you'd married her?

LEONARD

Oh, I couldn't help noticing it, of course, but it didn't seem to make so much difference to me then as it does now. I considered her beauty, and her property, and thought of nothing but the advantages of the match and the happiness I should have with her. But now these matters seem less important, and I do wish she could talk; that would be a real intellectual pleasure for me, and, what's more, a practical advantage for the household. What does a Judge need most in his house? Why, a good-looking wife, to receive the suitors pleasantly, and, by subtle suggestions, gently bring them to the point of making proper presents, so that their cases may receive—more careful attention. People need to be encouraged to make proper presents. A woman, by clever speech and prudent action, can get a good ham from one, and a roll of cloth from another; and make still another give poultry or wine. But this poor dumb thing Catherine gets nothing at all. While my fellow-judges have their kitchens and cellars and stables and store-rooms running over with good things, all thanks to their wives, I hardly get wherewithal to keep the pot boiling. You see, Master Adam Fumée, what I lose by having a dumb wife. I'm not worth half as much. . . . And the worst of it is, I'm losing my spirits, and almost my wits, with it all.

MASTER ADAM

There's no reason in that, now, your Honour. Just consider the thing closely, and you will find some advantages in your case as it stands, and no mean ones neither.

LEONARD

No, no, Master Adam; you don't understand. Think!—When I hold my wife in my arms—a woman as beautiful as the finest carved statue, at least so I think—and quite as silent, that I'm sure of—it makes me feel queer and uncanny; I even ask myself if I'm holding a graven image or a mechanical toy, or a magic doll made by a sorcerer, not a real human child of our Father in Heaven; sometimes, in the morning, I am tempted to jump out of bed to escape from bewitchment.

MASTER ADAM

What notions!

LEONARD

Worse yet! What with having a dumb wife, I'm going dumb myself. Sometimes I catch myself using signs, as she does. The other day, on the Bench, I even pronounced judgment in pantomime, and condemned a man to the galleys, just by dumb show and gesticulation.

MASTER ADAM

Enough! Say no more! I can see that a dumb wife may be a pretty poor conversationalist! There's not much fun in talking yourself, when you get no response.

LEONARD

Now you know the reason why I'm in low spirits.

MASTER ADAM

I won't contradict you; I admit that your reason is full and sufficient. But perhaps there's a remedy. Tell me: Is your wife deaf as well as dumb?

LEONARD

Catherine is no more deaf than you and I are; even less, I might say. She can hear the very grass growing.

A DUMB WIFE

MASTER ADAM

Then the case is not hopeless. When the doctors and surgeons and apothecaries succeed in making the deaf-and-dumb speak, their utterance is as poor as their ears; for they can't hear what they say themselves, any more than what's said to them. But it's quite different with the dumb who can hear. 'Tis but child's play for a doctor to untie their tongues. The operation is so simple that it's done every day to puppies that can't learn to bark. Must a countryman like me come to town to tell you that there's a famous doctor, just around the corner from your own house, in Buci Square, at the Sign of the Dragon, Master Simon Colline, who has made a reputation for loosing the tongues of the ladies of Paris? In a turn of the hand, he'll draw from your wife's lips a full flood of mellifluous speech, just as you'd turn on a spigot and let the water run forth like a sweet-purling brook.

LEONARD

Is this true, Master Adam? Aren't you deceiving me? Aren't you speaking as a lawyer in court?

MASTER ADAM

I'm speaking as a friend, and telling you the plain truth.

LEONARD

Then I'll send for this famous doctor—and that right away.

MASTER ADAM

As you please. . . . But before you call him in, you must reflect soberly, and consider what it's really best to do. For, take it all in all, though there are some disadvantages in having a dumb wife, there are some advantages, too. . . . Well, good day, your Honour, my dear old school-fellow. *(They go together to the street door.)* Remember, I'm truly your friend—and read over my statement, I beg you. If you give your just judgment in favor of the orphan girl robbed by her grasping guardian, you will have no cause to regret it.

LEONARD

Be back this afternoon, Master Adam Fumée; I will have my decision ready.

[*They bow low to each other. Exit* Master Adam.]

A DUMB WIFE

Scene II

Leonard; later Giles; later Catherine.

LEONARD

[*At the door, calling.*]

Giles! Giles! . . . The rogue never hears me; he is in the kitchen, as usual, upsetting the soup and the servant. He's a knave and a scoundrel. Giles! . . . Giles! . . . Here, you rapscallion! You reprobate! . . .

GILES

Present, your Honour.

LEONARD

(Taking him by the ear.)

Sirrah! Go straight to the famous doctor, Master Simon Colline, who lives in Buci Square, at the Sign of the Dragon, and tell him to come to my house at once, to treat a dumb woman. . . .

GILES

Yes, your Honour.

(Giles *starts off, running, to the right.*)

LEONARD

Go the nearest way, not round by the New Bridge, to watch the jugglers. I know you, you slow-poke; there's not such another cheat and loafer in ten counties.

> (GILES *comes back, slowly, across stage, and stops.*)

GILES

Sir, you wrong me. . . .

LEONARD

Be off! and bring the famous doctor back with you.

GILES

(Bolting off to the left.)
Yes, your Honour.

LEONARD

[*Going up and sitting down at the table, which is loaded with brief-bags.*]

I have fourteen verdicts to render to-day, besides the decree in the case of Master Adam Fumée's ward. And that is no small labour, because a decree, to do credit to the Judge,

A DUMB WIFE

must be cleverly worded, subtle, elegant, and adorned with all the ornaments both of style and of thought. The ideas must be pleasingly conceived and playfully expressed. Where should one show one's wit, if not in a verdict?

> *(The* WATERCRESS MAN *enters from the right and crosses to the left singing:* "Good watercress, fresh from the spring! Keeps you healthy and hearty! Six farthings a bunch. Six farthings a bunch." *When the watercress man is well on, enter the* CANDLE MAN *from left to right, singing:* "Candles! Cotton-wick candles! Burn bright as the stars!" *While he is passing,* CATHERINE *enters from the upper stairway door; she curtsies to the audience and then sits on the window-seat, embroidering. As the street-cries die away* LEONARD *looks up from his work at the table, and seeing Catherine, goes to her and kisses her as she rises to meet him. She makes a curtsy, kisses him in return, and listens with pleased attention.)*

Good morning, my love. . . . I didn't even hear you come down. You are like the fairy forms in the stories, that seem to glide upon air; or like the dreams which the gods, as poets tell, send down to happy mortals.

(CATHERINE *shows her pleasure in his compliments.*)

My love, you are a marvel of nature, and a triumph of art; you have all charms but speech. *(*CATHERINE *turns away sobbing slightly.)* Shouldn't you be glad to have that, too? *(She turns back, intensely interested.)* Shouldn't you be happy to let your lips utter all the pretty thoughts I can read in your eyes? Shouldn't you be pleased to show your wit? *(She waves her handkerchief in glee.)* Shouldn't you like to tell your husband how you love him? Wouldn't it be delightful to call him your treasure and sweetheart? Yes, surely! . . . *(They rise.* CATHERINE *is full of pleased animation.)*

Well, I've a piece of good news for you, my love. . . . A great doctor is coming here presently, who can make you talk. . . .

[CATHERINE *shows her satisfaction, dancing gracefully up and down.*]

He will untie your tongue and never hurt you a bit.

ENTER CATHERINE.

A DUMB WIFE 37

[CATHERINE'S *movements express charming and joyous impatience. A* BLIND MAN *goes by in the street playing a lively old-fashioned country dance. He stops and calls out in a doleful voice:* "Charity, for the love of God, good gentlemen and ladies." (LEONARD *motions him away, but* CATHERINE *pleads for him by her gestures, indicating that he is blind.* LEONARD *yields and goes back to his writing-table. She stands at the window listening while the blind man sings.*)]

THE BLIND MAN

There's lots of good fish in the sea,
  La dee ra, la dee ra;
Now who will come and fish with me?
  La dee ra, la dee ra;
Now who'll with me a-fishing go?
My dainty, dainty damsel, O!
Come fish the livelong day with me,
  La dee ra, la dee ra,
And who will then be caught?—we'll see!
  La dee ra, dee ra, day.

(Toward the end of the verse CATHERINE *glances at Leonard and sees that she is unobserved; she steals to the street door as the* BLIND MAN *begins the second verse there; during this verse she dances to him and frolics around the stage as he sings.)*

THE BLIND MAN

Along the rippling river's bank,
  La dee ra, la dee ra,
Along the wimpling water's bank,
  La dee ra, la dee ra,
Along the bank so shady O
I met the miller's lady, O
And danced with her the livelong day
  La dee ra, la dee ra,
And oh! I danced my heart away!
  La dee ra, dee ra, day.

[*The* BLIND MAN *stops playing and singing, and says, in a hollow and terrifying voice:* "Charity, for the love of God, good gentlemen and ladies."]

LEONARD

[*Who has been buried in his documents and noticed nothing, now drives the*

A DUMB WIFE

BLIND MAN *off the stage with objurgations.*]

Vagabond, robber, ruffian!

[*And throws a lot of brief-bags and books at his head; then speaks to* CATHERINE, *who has gone back to her place.*]

My love, since you came downstairs, I haven't been wasting my time; I have sentenced fourteen men and six women to the pillory; and distributed, among seventeen different people— *(He counts up)*—six, twenty-four, thirty-two, forty-four, forty-seven; and nine, fifty-six; and eleven, sixty-seven; and ten, seventy-seven; and eight, eighty-five; and twenty, a hundred and five—a hundred and five years in the galleys. Doesn't that make you realise the great power of a judge? How can I help feeling some pride in it?

[CATHERINE, *who has stopped her work, leans on the table, and smilingly watches her husband. Then she sits down on the table, which is covered with brief-bags.*]

LEONARD

[*Making as if to pull the bags from under her.*]

My love, you are hiding great criminals from my justice. Thieves and murderers. But I will not pursue them, their place of refuge is sacred.

> [A CHIMNEY SWEEP *passes in the street, calling:* "Sweep your chimneys, my ladies; sweep them clear and clean."]
>
> [LEONARD *and* CATHERINE *kiss across the table. But, seeing the* DOCTORS *arriving,* CATHERINE *runs off up the stairs.*]

Scene III

Leonard, Giles, Master Simon Colline, Master Jean Maugier, Two Attendants; later Master Serafin Dulaurier; later Alison.

(Enter, in formal procession, Giles, leading the line and imitating a trumpeter, then the two Doctors' Attendants, then Master Simon and Master Jean. The Attendants, one carrying the case of instruments, take their stand on either side of the door. The Doctor and Surgeon bow formally to the audience.)

GILES

Your Honour, here's the great doctor you sent for.

MASTER SIMON, *bowing*

Yes, I am Master Simon Colline himself. . . . And this is Master Jean Maugier, surgeon. You called for our services?

LEONARD

Yes, sir, to make a dumb woman speak.

MASTER SIMON

Good! We must wait for Master Serafin Dulaurier, apothecary. As soon as he comes we will proceed to operate according to our knowledge and understanding.

LEONARD

Ah! You really need an apothecary to make a dumb woman speak?

MASTER SIMON

Yes, sir; to doubt it is to show total ignorance of the relations of the organs to each other, and of their mutual interdependence. Master Serafin Dulaurier will soon be here.

MASTER JEAN MAUGIER

[*Suddenly bellowing out in stentorian tones.*]

Oh! how grateful we should be to learnèd doctors like Master Simon Colline, who labour to preserve us in health and comfort us in sickness. Oh! how worthy of praise and of blessings are these noble doctors who follow in their profession the rules of scientific theory and of long practice.

MASTER SIMON

[*Bowing slightly.*]

You are much too kind, Master Jean Maugier.

LEONARD

While we are waiting for the apothecary, won't you take some light refreshment, gentlemen?

MASTER SIMON

Most happy.

MASTER JEAN

Delighted.

LEONARD

Alison! . . . So then, Master Simon Colline, you will perform a slight operation and make my wife speak?

MASTER SIMON

Say, rather, I shall order the operation. I command, Master Jean Maugier executes. . . . Have you your instruments with you, Master Jean?

MASTER JEAN

Yes, Master.

[*(He claps his hands; the attendants run forward into the room, and, each hold-*

ing one side, they unfold the large cloth case of instruments and hold it up) disclosing a huge saw with two-inch teeth, and knives, pincers, scissors, a skewer, a bit-stock, an enormous bit, etc.]

LEONARD

I hope, sirs, you don't intend to use all those?

MASTER SIMON

One must never be caught unarmed by a patient.

(The attendants fold up the case and give it to Master Jean; then run back to their positions by the door, as ALISON, with a large tray, bottles, and glasses, enters from the kitchen.)

LEONARD

Will you drink, gentlemen?
(COLLINE and MAUGIER take glasses from ALISON and drink, after ALISON has kissed COLLINE's glass.)

MASTER SIMON

This light wine of yours is not half bad.

A DUMB WIFE

LEONARD

Very kind of you to say so. It's from my own vineyard.

MASTER SIMON

You shall send me a cask of it.

LEONARD

[*To* GILES, *who has poured himself a glass full to the brim.*]
I didn't tell you to drink, you reprobate.

MASTER JEAN

[*Looking out of the window.*]
Here is Master Serafin Dulaurier, the apothecary.
[*Enter* MASTER SERAFIN. *(He trots across the stage, stopping to bow to the audience.)*]

MASTER SIMON

(Peering into the street.)
And here is his mule! . . . Or no—'tis Master Serafin himself. You never can tell them

apart. *(MASTER SERAFIN joins the group in the room.)* Drink, Master Serafin. It is fresh from the cellar.

MASTER SERAFIN

Your good health, my Masters!

MASTER SIMON

[*To* ALISON.]
Pour freely, fair Hebe. Pour right, pour left, pour here, pour there. Whichever way she turns, she shows new charms. Are you not proud, my girl, of your trim figure?

ALISON

For all the good it does me, there is no reason to be proud of it. Charms are not worth much unless they are hidden in silk and brocade.

MASTER SERAFIN

Your good health, my Masters!
   [*They* ALL *drink, and make* ALISON *drink with them.*]

ALISON

You like to fool with us. But free gratis for nothing.

A DUMB WIFE

MASTER SIMON

Now we are all here, shall we go see the patient?

LEONARD

I will show you the way, gentlemen.

MASTER SIMON

After you, Master Maugier, you go first.

MASTER MAUGIER

(Glass in one hand, case of instruments in the other.)
I'll go first, since the place of honour is the rear. *(He crosses to the left, and goes behind the table toward the door, following Botal.)*

MASTER SIMON

After you, Master Serafin Dulaurier.
  [MASTER SERAFIN *follows Maugier, bottle in hand.* MASTER SIMON, *after stuffing a bottle into each pocket of his gown, and kissing the servant,* ALISON, *goes up stage, singing.*]
Then drink! and drink! and drink again!
Drink shall drown our care and pain.

*Good friends must drink before they part,
To warm the cockles of the heart!*
  [ALISON, *after cuffing* GILES, *who was trying to kiss her, goes up last.*]
  (ALL *sing in chorus as they go out by the right upper door:*)
Then drink! and drink! and drink again!

[*End of ACT I*]

ACT II

Scene:—the same. Four or five hours have elapsed.

Scene I

LEONARD, MASTER ADAM.

MASTER ADAM

Good afternoon, your Honour. How are you this afternoon?

LEONARD

Well, fairly well. And how are you?

MASTER ADAM

Well as can be. Excuse my besieging you, your Honour, my dear comrade. Have you looked into the case of my young ward who's been robbed by her guardian?

LEONARD

Not yet, Master Adam Fumée. . . . But what's that you say? You've been robbing your ward?

MASTER ADAM

No, no, never think it, your Honour. I said "my" out of pure interest in her. But I am not her guardian, thank God! I'm her lawyer. And, if she gets back her estate, which is no small estate neither, then I shall be her husband; yes, I've had the foresight to make her fall in love with me already. And so, I shall be greatly obliged to you if you'll examine her case at the earliest possible moment. All you have to do is to read the statement I gave you; that contains everything you need to know about the case.

LEONARD

Your statement is there, Master Adam, on my table. I should have looked through it already, if I hadn't been so besieged. But I've been entertaining the flower of the medical faculty here. *(Suddenly seizing him by the shoulders and shaking him.)* 'Twas your advice brought this trouble upon me.

A DUMB WIFE

MASTER ADAM

Why, what do you mean?

LEONARD

I sent for the famous doctor you told me about, Master Simon Colline. He came, with a surgeon and an apothecary; he examined my wife, Catherine, from head to foot, to see if she was dumb. Then, the surgeon cut my dear Catherine's tongue-ligament, the apothecary gave her a pill—and she spoke.

MASTER ADAM

She spoke? Did she need a pill, to speak?

LEONARD

Yes, because of the interdependence of the organs.

MASTER ADAM

Oh! Ah! . . . Anyhow, the main point is, she spoke. And what did she say?

LEONARD

She said: "Bring me my looking-glass!" And, seeing me quite overcome by my feelings, she added, "You old goose, you shall give me a new satin gown and a velvet-trimmed cape for my birthday."

MASTER ADAM

And she kept on talking?

LEONARD

She hasn't stopped yet.

MASTER ADAM

And yet you don't thank me for my advice; you don't thank me for having sent you to that wonderful doctor? Aren't you overjoyed to hear your wife speak?

LEONARD

[*Sourly.*]
Yes, certainly. I thank you with all my heart, Master Adam Fumée, and I am overjoyed to hear my wife speak.

MASTER ADAM

No! You do not show as much satisfaction as you ought to. There is something you are keeping back—something that's worrying you.

A DUMB WIFE 53

LEONARD

Where did you get such a notion?

MASTER ADAM

From your face. . . . What is bothering you? Isn't your wife's speech clear?

LEONARD

Yes, it's clear—and abundant. I must admit, its abundance would be a trial to me if it kept up at the rate which it started at.

MASTER ADAM

Ah! . . . I feared *that* beforehand, your Honour. But you mustn't be cast down too soon. Perhaps this flood of words will ebb. It is the first overflow of a spring too long bottled up. . . . My best congratulations, your Honour. My ward's name is Ermeline de la Garandière. Don't forget her name; show her favour, and you will find proper gratitude. I will be back later in the day.

LEONARD

Master Adam Fumée, I will look into your case at once.

[*Exit* MASTER ADAM FUMÉE.]

Scene II

Leonard; later Catherine.

(Catherine *is heard off stage singing the Blind Man's song; Leonard starts, shakes his head, hurries to his writing-table, and sits down to work. Catherine, still singing, enters gaily, and goes to him at the table.*)

LEONARD

[*Reading.*]
"Statement, on behalf of Ermeline-Jacinthe-Marthe de la Garandière, gentlewoman."

CATHERINE

(*Standing behind his chair, and first finishing her song: "La dee ra, dee ra, day", then speaking with great volubility.*)
What are you doing, my dear? You seem busy. You work too much. (*She goes to the window-seat and takes up her embroidery.*) Aren't you afraid it will make you ill? You

must rest once in a while. Why don't you tell me what you are doing, dear?

LEONARD

My love, I . . .

CATHERINE

Is it such a great secret? Can't I know about it?

LEONARD

My love, I . . .

CATHERINE

If it's a secret, don't tell me.

LEONARD

Won't you give me a chance to answer? I am examining a case and preparing to draw up a verdict on it.

CATHERINE

Is drawing up a verdict so very important?

LEONARD

Most certainly it is. (CATHERINE *sits at the window singing and humming to herself, and looking out.*) In the first place, people's honour, their liberty, and sometimes even their life, may depend on it; and furthermore, the Judge must show therein both the depth of his thought and the finish of his style.

CATHERINE

Then examine your case and prepare your verdict, my dear. I'll be silent.

LEONARD

That's right. . . . "Ermeline-Jacinthe-Marthe de la Garandière, gentlewoman . . ."

CATHERINE

My dear, which do you think would be more becoming to me, a damask gown, or a velvet suit with a Turkish skirt?

LEONARD

I don't know, I . . .

CATHERINE

I think a flowered satin would suit my age best, especially a light-coloured one, with a *small* flower pattern.

"Now we are all here, shall we go see the patient?"

LEONARD

Perhaps so. But . . .

CATHERINE

And don't you think, my dear, that it is quite improper to have a hoop-skirt very full? Of course, a skirt must have *some* fullness . . . or else you don't seem dressed at all; so, we mustn't let it be scanty. But, my dear, you wouldn't want me to have room enough to hide a pair of lovers under my hoops, now would you? That fashion won't last, I'm sure; some day the court ladies will give it up, and then every woman in town will make haste to follow their example. Don't you think so?

LEONARD

Yes! Yes! But . . .

CATHERINE

Now, about high heels. . . . They must be made just right. A woman is judged by her foot-gear—you can always tell a real fine lady by her shoes. You agree with me, don't you, dear?

LEONARD

Yes, yes, *yes*, but . . .

CATHERINE

Then write out your verdict. I shan't say another word.

LEONARD

That's right.
[*Reading, and making notes.*]
"Now, the guardian of the said young lady, namely, Hugo Thomas of Piédeloup, gentleman, stole from the said young lady her——"

CATHERINE

My dear, if one were to believe the wife of the Chief Justice of Montbadon, the world has grown very corrupt; it is going to the bad; young men nowadays don't marry; they prefer to hang about rich old ladies; and meanwhile the poor girls are left to wither on their maiden stalks. Do you think it's as bad as all that? Do answer me, dear.

LEONARD

My darling, won't you please be silent one moment? Or go and talk somewhere else? I'm all at sea.

CATHERINE

There, there, dear; don't worry. I shan't say another word! Not a word!

LEONARD

Good!
[*Writing.*]
"The said Piédeloup, gentleman, counting both hay crops and apple crops . . ."

CATHERINE

My dear, we shall have for supper to-night some minced mutton and what's left of that goose one of your suitors gave us. Tell me, is that enough? Shall you be satisfied with it? I hate being mean, and like to set a good table, but what's the use of serving courses which will only be sent back to the pantry untouched? The cost of living is getting higher all the time. Chickens, and salads, and meats, and fruit have all gone up so, it will soon be cheaper to order dinner sent in by a caterer.

LEONARD

I beg you . . .
   [*Writing.*]
"An orphan by birth . . ."

CATHERINE

Yes, that's what we're coming to. No home life any more. You'll see. Why, a capon, or a partridge, or a hare, cost less all stuffed and roasted than if you buy them alive at the market. That is because the cook-shops buy in large quantities and get a big discount; so they can sell to us at a profit. I don't say we ought to get our regular meals from the cook-shop. We can do our everyday plain cooking at home, and it's better to; but when we invite people in, or give a formal dinner party, then it saves time and money to have the dinner sent in. Why, at less than an hour's notice, the cook-shops and cake-shops will get you up a dinner for a dozen, or twenty, or fifty people; the cook-shop will send in meat and poultry, the caterer will send galantines and sauces and relishes, the pastry-cook will send pies and tarts and sweets and desserts; and it's all so convenient. Now, don't you think so yourself, Leonard?

LEONARD

Please, please!
> (LEONARD *tries to write through the following speech, murmuring:* "An orphan by birth, a capon by birth, an olla podrida," *etc.*)

CATHERINE

It's no wonder everything goes up. People are getting more extravagant every day. If they are entertaining a friend, or even a relative, they don't think they can do with only three courses, soup, meat, and dessert. No, they have to have meats in five or six different styles, with so many sauces, or dressings, or pasties, that it's a regular olla podrida. Now, don't you think that is going too far, my dear? For my part I just cannot understand how people can take pleasure in stuffing themselves with so many kinds of food. Not that I despise a good table; why, I'm even a bit of an epicure myself. "Not too plenty, but dainty," suits *my* taste. Now, what I like best of all is capons' kidneys with artichoke hearts. But you, Leonard, I suspect you have a weakness for tripe and sausages. Oh, fie! Oh, fie! How can anyone enjoy sausages?

LEONARD

[*His head in his hands.*]
I shall go mad! I know I shall go mad.

CATHERINE

(Running to the table behind him.)
My dear, I just shan't say another word—not a single word. For I can see that my chattering *might* possibly disturb your work.

LEONARD

If you would only do as you say!

CATHERINE

(Returning to her place.)
I shan't even open my lips.

LEONARD

Splendid!

CATHERINE

(Busily embroidering.)
You see, dear, I'm not saying another word.

LEONARD

Yes.

CATHERINE

I'm letting you work in perfect peace and quiet.

LEONARD

Yes.

CATHERINE

And write out your verdict quite undisturbed. Is it almost done?

LEONARD

It never will be—if you don't keep still.
   [*Writing.*]
"Item, One hundred twenty pounds a year, which the said unworthy guardian stole from the poor orphan girl . . ."

CATHERINE

Listen! Ssh-sh! Listen! Didn't you hear a cry of fire? *(Leonard runs to the window, looks out, and then shakes his head at Catherine.)* I thought I did. But perhaps I may have been mistaken. Is there anything so terrifying as a fire? Fire is even worse than water. Last year I saw the houses on Exchange Bridge burn up. What confusion! What havoc! The people threw their furniture into the river, and jumped out of the windows. They didn't know what they were about; you see, fear drove them out of their senses.

LEONARD

Lord, have mercy upon me!

CATHERINE

Oh! What makes you groan so, dear? *Tell* me, tell me what is the matter?

LEONARD

I can't endure it another minute.

A DUMB WIFE

CATHERINE

You must rest, Leonard. You mustn't work so hard. It isn't reasonable. You have no right to . . .

LEONARD

Will you never be still?

CATHERINE

Now, don't be cross, dear. I'm not saying a word.

LEONARD

Would to Heaven!
> (MADAME DE LA BRUINE, *followed by her footman, crosses the stage during the following speech.*)

CATHERINE

[*Looking out of the window.*]
Oh! Here comes Madame de la Bruine, the attorney's wife! She's got on a silk-lined hood and a heavy puce-coloured cape over her brocade gown. And she has a lackey with a face like a smoked herring. Leonard, she's looking this way; I believe she's coming to call. Hurry and arrange the chairs and bring up an

armchair for her; we must show people proper respect according to their rank and station. She is stopping at our door. No, she's going on. She's gone on. Perhaps I was mistaken. Perhaps it was somebody else. You can't be sure about recognising people. But if it wasn't she, it was somebody like her, and even very much like her. Now I think of it, I'm sure it was she, there simply couldn't be another woman in Paris so like Madame de la Bruine. My dear. . . My dear. . . Would you have liked to have Madame de la Bruine call on us?

[*She sits down on his table.*]

I know you don't like rattle-tongued women; it's lucky for you that you didn't marry *her;* she jabbers like a magpie; she does nothing but gabble from morning to night. What a chatterbox! And sometimes she tells stories which are not to her credit.

[LEONARD, *driven beyond endurance, climbs up on his step-ladder and sits down on one of the middle steps, and tries to write there.*]

In the first place, she always gives you a list of all the presents her husband has received. It's a dreadful bore to hear her tell them over.

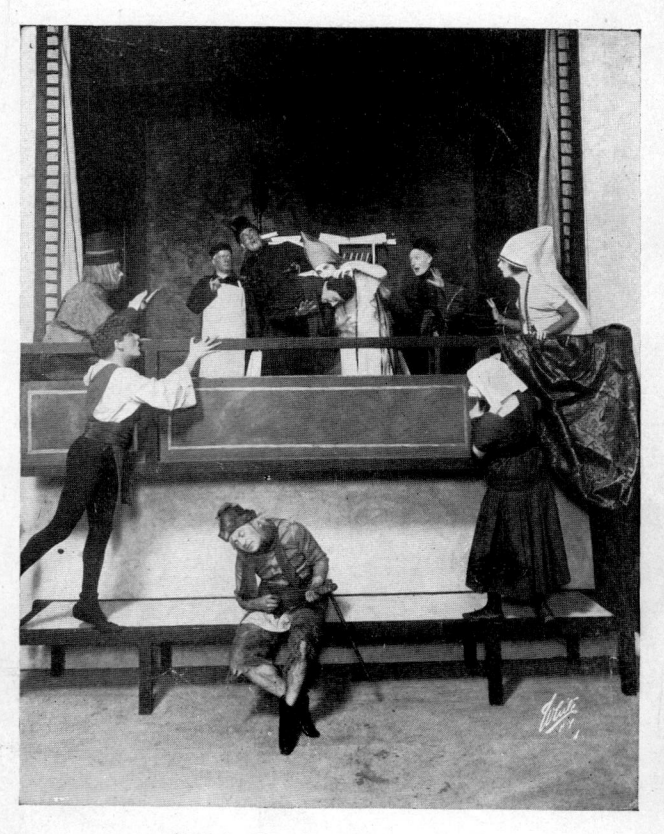

"Oh! She has bitten me!"

A DUMB WIFE

[*She climbs up on the other side of the double step-ladder and sits down opposite Leonard.*]

What is it to us, if the Attorney de la Bruine receives presents of game, or flour, or fresh fish, or even a sugar-loaf? But Madame de la Bruine takes good care *not* to tell you that one day her husband received a great Amiens pasty, and when he opened it he found nothing but an enormous pair of horns.

LEONARD

My head will burst!

[*He takes refuge on top of one of the cabinets, with his writing-case and papers.*]

CATHERINE

[*At the top of the ladder.*]

And did you see my fine lady, who's really no lady at all, wearing an embroidered cape, just like any princess? Don't you think it's ridiculous! But there! Nowadays everybody dresses above his station, men as well as women. Your court secretaries try to pass for gentlemen; they wear gold chains and jewelry, and feathers in their hats; all the same, anyone can tell what they are.

LEONARD

[*On top of his cupboard.*]

I've got to the point where I can't answer for the consequences; I feel capable of committing any crime.

[*Calling.*]

Giles! Giles! Giles! The scoundrel! Giles! Alison! Giles! Giles!

[*Enter* GILES.]

Go quick and find the famous Doctor in Buci Square, Master Simon Colline, and tell him to come back here at once for a matter far more needful and urgent than before.

GILES

Yes, your Honour.

[*Exit.*]

CATHERINE

What's the matter, my dear? You seem excited. Perhaps the air is close. No? It's the east wind, then, don't you think?—or the fish you ate for dinner?

A DUMB WIFE

LEONARD

[*Frantically gesticulating on top of his cupboard.*]

Non omnia possumus omnes. It is the office of servants to clean crockery, of mercers to measure ribbon, of monks to beg, of birds to drop dirt around everywhere, and of women to cackle and chatter like mad. Oh! How I regret, you saucy baggage, that I had your tongue loosed. Don't you worry, though—the famous doctor shall soon make you more dumb than ever you were.

[*He catches up armfuls of the brief-bags which are piled on his cupboard of refuge, and throws them at* CATHERINE's *head; she jumps nimbly down from the ladder and runs off in terror, crying:*]

CATHERINE

Help! Murder! My husband's gone mad! Help! help!

LEONARD

Alison! Alison!

[*Enter* ALISON.]

ALISON

What a life! Sir, have you turned murderer?

LEONARD

Alison, follow her, stay by her, and don't let her come down. As you value your life, Alison, don't let her come down. For if I hear another word from her, I shall go raving mad, and God knows what I might do to her—and to you. Go! Off with you!

[ALISON *goes upstairs.*]

Scene III

Leonard, Master Adam, Mlle. de la Garandière, and a Lackey carrying a basket.
> (Leonard *is still on top of the cabinet or book-case.* Master Adam *and* Mlle. de la Garandière *climb up on each side of the step-ladder. The* Lackey, *with an enormous basket on his head, kneels in front, centre.*)

MASTER ADAM

Permit me, your Honour, with the object of softening your heart and arousing your pity, to present before you this young orphan girl, despoiled by a grasping guardian, who implores you for justice. Her eyes will speak to your heart more eloquently than my voice. Mlle. de la Garandière brings you her prayers and her tears; she adds thereunto one ham, two duck pies, a goose, and two goslings. She ventures to hope in exchange for a favouring verdict.

LEONARD

Mademoiselle, you arouse my interest. . . . Have you anything to add in defence of your case?

MLLE. DE LA GARANDIÈRE

You are only too kind, sir; I must rest my case on what my lawyer has just said.

LEONARD

That is all?

MLLE. DE LA GARANDIÈRE

Yes, sir.

LEONARD

She knows how to speak—and to stop. The poor orphan touches my heart.

[*To the* LACKEY.]

Carry that package to the pantry.

[*Exit* LACKEY.]

[*To* MASTER ADAM.]

Master Adam, when you came in, I was just drawing up the decree which I shall presently render in this young lady's case.

[*He starts to come down from his cabinet.*]

"Mademoiselle, you arouse my interest."

A DUMB WIFE

MASTER ADAM

What, up on that cupboard?

LEONARD

I don't know where I am; my head is going round and round. Do you want to hear the decree? I need to read it over myself.
[*Reading.*]
"Whereas, Mlle. de la Garandière, spinster, and an orphan by birth, did fraudulently, deceitfully, and with injurious inter steal, filch, and subtract from her lawful guardian, Squire Piédeloup, gentleman, ten loads of hay and eighty pounds of fresh-water fish, and whereas, there is nothing so terrifying as a fire, and whereas, the State's Attorney did receive an Amiens pasty in which were two great horns . . ."

MASTER ADAM

What in Heaven's name are you reading?

LEONARD

Don't ask me. I don't know myself. I think my brains have been brayed in a mortar, for two hours running, by the very devil himself for a pestle. *(He breaks down and weeps on their shoulders.)* I'm a driveling idiot. . . . And all your fault, too, Master Adam Fumée. . . . If that fine doctor of yours hadn't restored my wife's speech . . .

MASTER ADAM

Don't blame me, Master Leonard. I forewarned you. I told you right enough, that you must think twice before untying a woman's tongue.

LEONARD

Ah, Master Adam Fumée, how I long for the time when my Catherine was dumb. No! Nature has no scourge more fearsome than a rattle-tongued female. . . . But I count on the doctors to recall their cruel gift. I have sent for them. Here's the surgeon now.

A DUMB WIFE

Scene IV

The Same, Master Jean Maugier; later Master Simon Colline and Master Serafin Dulaurier, followed by Two Apothecary's Boys.

MASTER JEAN MAUGIER

Your Honour, I bid you good day. Here is Master Simon Colline coming forward upon his mule, followed by Master Serafin Dulaurier, apothecary. About him crowds the adoring populace: chambermaids, trussing up their petticoats, and scullions with hampers on their heads, form his escort of honour.

[*Enter* Master Simon Colline *and* His Suite.]

Oh! how justly does Master Simon Colline command the admiration of the people when he goes through the city clad in his doctor's robe, his square cap, his cassock and bands. Oh! how grateful we should be to those noble doctors who labour to preserve us in health and comfort us in sickness. Ohhhh! how . . .

MASTER SIMON

[*To* MASTER JEAN MAUGIER.]
Have done; 'tis enough.

LEONARD

Master Simon Colline, I was in haste to see you. I urgently beg for your services.

MASTER SIMON

For yourself? What is your disease? Where is the pain?

LEONARD

No! For my wife; the one who was dumb.

MASTER SIMON

Has she any trouble now?

LEONARD

None at all. I have all the trouble now.

MASTER SIMON

What? The trouble is with you, and it's your wife you want cured?

A DUMB WIFE

LEONARD

Master Simon Colline, she talks too much. You should have given her speech, but not so much speech. Since you've cured her of her dumbness, she drives me mad. I cannot bear another word from her. I've called you in to make her dumb again.

MASTER SIMON

'Tis impossible!

LEONARD

What's that? You can't take away the power of speech which you gave her?

MASTER SIMON

No! That I cannot do. My skill is great, but it stops short of that.

(LEONARD in despair turns to each of them in succession.)

MASTER JEAN MAUGIER

We cannot do it.

MASTER SERAFIN

Our greatest efforts would have not the slightest result.

MASTER SIMON

We have medicines to make women speak; we have none to make them keep silence.

LEONARD

You haven't? Is that your last word? You drive me to despair.

MASTER SIMON

Alas, your Honour! *(He advances to the centre, claps his hands for attention, and declaims.)* There is no elixir, balm, magisterium, opiate, unguent, ointment, local application, electuary, nor panacea, that can cure the excess of glottal activity in woman. Treacle and orvietano would be without virtue, and all the herbs described by Dioscorides would have no effect.

LEONARD

Can this be true?

MASTER SIMON

Sir, you dare not so offend me as to doubt it.

A DUMB WIFE

LEONARD

Then I am a ruined man. There's nothing left for me to do but tie a stone around my neck and jump into the Seine. *(He rushes to the window and tries to jump out, but is held back by the doctors.)* I cannot live in this hubbub. *(The doctors drag him back, set him down, and, with* Master Adam, *stand in a circle in front of him.)* If you don't want me to drown myself straightway, then you doctors must find me some cure.

MASTER SIMON

There is none, I tell you, for your wife. But there might be one for you, if you would consent to take it.

LEONARD

You give me a little hope. Explain it, for Heaven's sake.

MASTER SIMON

For the clack of a wife, there's but one cure in life. Let her husband be deaf. 'Tis the only relief.

LEONARD

What do you mean?

MASTER SIMON

Just what I say.

MASTER ADAM

Don't you understand? That's the finest discovery yet. Since he can't make your wife dumb, this great doctor offers to make you deaf.

LEONARD

Make me really deaf? Oh! . . .
(He starts to rise, but is pushed back by MASTER SIMON, *who stands directly in front of him.)*

MASTER SIMON

Certainly. I can cure you at once, and for all time, of your wife's verbal hypertrophy, by means of cophosis.

LEONARD

By cophosis? What is cophosis?

MASTER SIMON

'Tis what is vulgarly called deafness. Do you see any disadvantages in becoming deaf?

LEONARD

Certainly I do!

MASTER JEAN MAUGIER

You think so?

MASTER SERAFIN

For instance?

MASTER SIMON

You are a Judge. What disadvantage is there in a Judge's being deaf?

MASTER ADAM

None at all. Believe me; I am a practicing lawyer. There is none at all.

MASTER SIMON

What harm could come to justice thereby?

MASTER ADAM

No harm at all. Quite the contrary. Master Leonard Botal could then hear neither lawyers nor prosecutors, and so would run no risk of being deceived by a lot of lies.

LEONARD

That's true.

MASTER ADAM

He will judge all the better.

LEONARD

May be so.

MASTER ADAM

Never doubt it.

LEONARD

But how do you perform this . . .

MASTER JEAN MAUGIER

This cure.

MASTER SIMON

Cophosis, vulgarly called deafness, may be brought about in several ways. It is produced either by otorrhœa, or by sclerosis of the ear, or by otitis, or else by anchylosis of the ossicles. But these various means are long and painful.

LEONARD

I reject them! . . . I reject them absolutely.

MASTER SIMON

You are right. It is far better to induce cophosis by means of a certain white powder which I have in my medicine-case; a pinch of it, placed in the ear, is enough to make you as deaf as Heaven when it's angry, or as deaf as a post.

LEONARD

Many thanks, Master Simon Colline; keep your powder. I will not be made deaf.

MASTER SIMON

What? You won't be made deaf? What? You refuse cophosis? You decline the cure which you begged for just now? Ah, 'tis a case but too common, and one calculated to make a judicious physician grieve, to see a recalcitrant patient refuse the salutary medicament . . .

MASTER JEAN MAUGIER

And flee from the care, which would cure all his ailments . . .

MASTER SERAFIN

And decline to be healed. Oh!

MASTER ADAM

Do not decide too quickly, Master Leonard Botal; do not deliberately reject this slight affliction which will save you from far greater torment.

LEONARD

No! I will not be deaf; I'll have none of your powder.

Scene V

The Same, Alison; later Catherine.

ALISON

[*Rushes in from the stairs, stopping her ears.*]

I can't stand it. My head will burst. No human creature can stay and listen to such a clatter. There's no stopping her. I feel as if I'd been caught in the mill-wheel for two mortal hours.

(Catherine *is heard off stage singing the blind man's song.*)

LEONARD

Wretch! Don't let her come down. Alison! Giles! Lock her in.

MASTER ADAM

Oh! Sir!

MLLE. DE LA GARANDIÈRE

Oh! Sir, can your heart be so cruel as to want to lock the poor lady up all alone?

(Catherine is heard singing again. Leonard starts for the ladder, and climbs it as she enters.)

CATHERINE

What a fine large assembly! I am your humble servant, gentlemen.
[*She curtsies.*]

MASTER SIMON COLLINE

Well, madam? Aren't you pleased with us? Didn't we do our work well in loosing your tongue?

CATHERINE

Fairly well, sirs; and I'm truly grateful to you. At first, to be sure, I could speak but haltingly, and bring out only a few words; now, however, I have some degree of facility; but I use it with great moderation, for a garrulous wife is a scourge in the house. Yes, gentlemen, I should be in despair if you could so much as suspect me of loquacity, or if you could think for a moment that any undue desire to talk could get hold on me. *(Leonard, on top of the cabinet, laughs wildly.)* And so, I beg you to let me justify myself here and now in the eyes of my husband, who, for some inconceivable reason, has become prejudiced against me, and taken it into his head that my conversation bothered him while he was drawing up a decree. . . . Yes, a decree in favour of an orphan girl deprived of her father and mother in the flower of her youth. But no matter for that. *(She crosses to the ladder and starts to go up one side of it.* LEONARD *climbs down the other side, goes first to one doctor, then to another, and finally sits down on the bench in front of the table.)* I was sitting beside him and hardly saying a single word to him. My only speech was my presence. Can a husband object to that? Can he take it ill when his wife stays with him and seeks to enjoy his company, as she ought?

(She goes to her husband and sits down beside him. During the rest of the speech all those present, one after another, sink down in exhaustion at listening to her.)

The more I think of it, the less I can understand your impatience. What can have caused it? You must stop pretending it was my talka-

A DUMB WIFE 87

tiveness. That idea won't hold water one moment. My dear, you must have some grievance against me which I know nothing about; I *beg* you to tell me what it is. You *owe* me an explanation, and as soon as I find out what displeased you I will see to it that you have no reason to complain of the same thing again—if only you'll tell me what it is. For I am eager to save you from the slightest reason for dissatisfaction. My mother used to say: "Between husband and wife, there should be no secrets." And she was quite right. Married people have only too often brought down terrible catastrophes on themselves or their households just because they didn't tell each other everything. That is what happened to the Chief Justice of Beaupréau's wife. To give her husband a pleasant surprise, she shut up a little sucking pig in a chest in her room. Her husband heard it squealing, and thought it was a lover, so he out with his sword and ran his wife through the heart, without even waiting to hear the poor lady's explanation. You can imagine his surprise and despair when he opened the chest. And that shows you must never have secrets, even for good reasons. My dear, you can speak freely before these gentlemen. I know I have done nothing wrong, so whatever you say can only prove the more clearly how innocent I am.

LEONARD

[*Who has for some time been trying in vain by gestures and exclamations to stop* CATHERINE'S *flow of words, and has been showing signs of extreme impatience.*]

The powder! Give me the powder! Master Simon Colline, your powder—your white powder, for God's sake!

MASTER SIMON

Never was a deafness-producing powder more needed, that's sure. Be so kind as to sit down, your Honour. Master Serafin Dulaurier will inject the cophosis powder in your ears.

(*The doctors crowd about* LEONARD, *and inject the powder first in one ear and then in the other.*)

A DUMB WIFE

MASTER SERAFIN

Gladly, sir, gladly.

MASTER SIMON

There! 'Tis done.

CATHERINE

[*To* MASTER ADAM FUMÉE.]
Master Adam, you are a lawyer. Make my husband hear reason. Tell him that he must listen to me, that it's unheard of to condemn a wife without letting her state her case, tell him it's not right to throw brief-bags at your wife's head—yes, he threw brief-bags at my head— unless you are forced to it by some very strong feeling or reason. . . . Or no!—no, I'll tell him myself.

[*To* LEONARD.]
My dear, answer me, have I ever failed you in anything? Am I a naughty woman? Am I a bad wife? No, I have been faithful to my duty; I may even say I have loved my duty . . .

LEONARD

[*His face expressing beatitude, as he calmly twirls his thumbs.*]

'Tis delicious. I can't hear a thing.

CATHERINE

Listen to me, Leonard, I love you tenderly. I will open my heart to you. I am not one of those light, frivolous women who are afflicted or consoled by airy nothings, and amused by trifles. *(She puts her arms about him and they rock back and forth,* LEONARD *grinning from ear to ear.)* I need companionship. I need to be understood. That is my nature—I was born so. When I was only seven years old I had a little dog, a little yellow dog. . . . But you're not listening to me . . .

MASTER SIMON

Madam, he can't listen to you, or to anyone else. He can't hear.

CATHERINE

What do you mean he can't hear?

MASTER SIMON

I mean just that. He can't hear, as the result of a cure he has just taken.

(The BLIND MAN *is heard again, playing the same air.)*

"'Tis delicious! I can't hear a thing."

MASTER SERAFIN

A cure which has produced in him a sweet and pleasant cophosis.

CATHERINE

I'll make him hear, I tell you.

MASTER SIMON

No, you won't, madam; it can't be done.

CATHERINE

You shall see.

[*To her husband, affectionately.*]

My dear, my beloved, my pretty one, my sweetheart, my better-half. . . . You don't hear me?

[*She shakes him.*]

You monster, you Herod, you Bluebeard, you old cuckold.

LEONARD

I can't hear her with my ears, but I hear her only too well with my arms, and with my shoulders and back.

MASTER SIMON

She is going mad.

MASTER MAUGIER

She has gone mad! Stark, staring mad!

LEONARD

Oh! How can I get away? *(CATHERINE bites his neck.)* Oh! She has bitten me, I feel myself going mad, too.

> *(The BLIND MAN has come forward, playing and singing the first verse of his song. Meanwhile CATHERINE and LEONARD go singing and dancing about, and bite the others, who likewise go mad and sing and dance wildly, all at the front of the stage. The other characters of the play come in—the CANDLE MAN, CHIMNEY SWEEP, MADAME DE LA BRUINE, etc.; all are caught and bitten, and join in the song and the dance, which resolves itself into the old-fashioned country "right and left", as they sing the second verse.)*

ALL

Along the rippling river's bank,
La dee ra, la dee ra,

A DUMB WIFE

Along the wimpling water's bank,
  La dee ra, la dee ra,
Along the bank so shady O
I met the miller's lady O
And danced with her the livelong day,
  La dee ra, la dee ra,
And oh! I danced my heart away,
  La dee ra, dee ra, day.
  (As LEONARD BOTAL *reaches the centre of the front stage, the dance stops a moment for him to say to the audience:)*

LEONARD

Good gentlemen and ladies, we pray you to forgive the author all his faults.
  (The dance re-commences, and as the curtain falls all dance off left or right, singing the refrain.)

ALL, *diminuendo*

I danced with her the livelong day,
  La dee ra, la dee ra,
And oh! I danced my heart away,
  La dee ra, dee ra, day.

CURTAIN

BLIND MAN'S SONG AND DANCE

(To the tune of "Dargason.")

There's lots of good fish in the sea, La deera, la dee ra, Now who will come and fish with me? La deera, la dee ra, Now who with me will fish-ing go, My dain-ty, dain-ty dam-sel, O, Come fish the live-long day with me, And who will then be caught, we'll see, La deera, la deera, La deera, dee-ra day.

DRINKING SONG

(To the tune of "The Beggar.")
See Folk Songs from Somerset, No. 82.

Then drink and drink and drink a-gain, And drown all care and pain, Good friends must drink be-fore they part, To warm the cock-les of the heart.

CHORUS.

Let the back and the sides go bare, my boys, Let the hands and the feet gang cold But give to the bel-ly, boys, wine e-nough, Whether it be new or old.

STREET CRIES

Chickweed.

Chick - weed, Chick weed, good bird-seed, good bird-seed, good bird-seed for sale.

Sweeps.

Sweep, Sweep, your chim - neys my la dies, Sweep them clear and clean.

Water Cress.

Good wa-ter cress, fresh from the spring, keeps you healthy and hearty, Six farthings a bunch, Six farth-ings a bunch.

Candles.

Can - dles, Cot-ton-wick can-dles, burn bright as the stars.